Happy Birthday #1

To Sloane —
Bee careful what
ewe ask four...

MISS SPELL
IS A CLEVER LITTLE PRINCESS.

SHE TURNED FROGGY

INTO A PRINCE

AND BACK.

SHE TURNED MICE AND RABBITS

INTO BUTLERS AND MAIDS.

SHE TURNED BLACKBIRDS
INTO GNOMES AND SET THEM LOOSE
ON THE GARDENERS.

THIS MADE QUEEN SPELL
A LITTLE ANGRY.

ONE MORNING, MISS SPELL
FOUND A NOTE IN THE GARDEN.

Dear Miss Spell,

You should only
use your magic
for what is
write.
Signed,
Froggy
(formerly known as Prince)

THIS GAVE HER A VERY CLEVER IDEA.

WITHIN A FEW DAYS, MAILMAN MAX
PEDALED UP THE HILL TO THE
CASTLE AND PLOPPED A SMALL
BAG ONTO HER DOORSTEP.

SHE
EAGERLY
READ:

Dear Miss Spell,
I wish for an
aunt farm to
fill my whole
backyard!
Love,
Bianca

MISS SPELL
WAS DELIGHTED!
"AUNT FARM,
HUH?"

THE NEXT MORNING,
BIANCA PEERED OUT HER
WINDOW AND GASPED.

ONE WEEK LATER, MAILMAN MAX DROVE
A DUMP TRUCK TO MISS SPELL'S CASTLE.

MISS SPELL
PICKED A
LETTER,
SHRIEKING
JOYFULLY,
"THIS'LL BE
FUN!"

Dear Miss Spell,
I'm tired of wigs!
I wish for
piles of hare
upon my head.
Sincerely,
Stanley Snorts

SHE
GIGGLED
THINKING OF
STANLEY'S HEAD
OF HARE.

SOON AFTER, MAILMAN MAX
DROVE A SEMI-TRUCK UP THE
HILL TO THE CASTLE.

SHE SEARCHED
THEN
SQUEALED,
"AHA!"

Dear Miss Spell,

I've got a secret:
I'm a timid knight in a scary job.
The king has ordered me
to sleigh the forest dragon.
Will you please
sleigh him for me?

Secretly,
Sir Shakesalot

MONSTROUSLY MAMMOTH
MAILMAN MAX'S
MAIL MOVER

"HO HO HO!
I'LL SLEIGH
THAT DRAGON!"
SHE SAID.

IT SEEMED THE CLEVER MISS SPELL
HAD BEEN A VERY NAUGHTY
LITTLE PRINCESS.

"A TOE WITH TIRES?!"

"AUNTS MAKING RACKET?!"

"THE DRAGON'S CAUSING
A TRAFFIC JAM!"

THAT VERY AFTERNOON
MAILMAN MAX SHOWED
QUEEN SPELL HIS PLAN
TO STOP THE RUCKUS.

QUEEN SPELL
WAS DELIGHTED!

A FEW DAYS LATER, MAILMAN MAX RODE
HIS UNICYCLE UP THE HILL AND DELIVERED
A SINGLE CARD TO MISS SPELL.

Miss Spell, this must stop!!!
Bianca meant ant not aunt.
Baxter meant tow not toe.
Stanley wanted hair not a hare.
The village is at a total standstill.
The giant sleigh is blocking traffic!
Villagers want the knight
to slay the dragon.

Now my wish :
You be a deer
and change everything back
the way it was once upon a time . . .

Exhaustedly yours,
Mailman Max

MISS SPELL
GIGGLED,
"IMAGINE ME,
A DEER?!"
AND AS
SHE SAID IT
ALOUD, THERE
WAS A
SUDDEN

POOF!

MISS SPELL LOOKED DOWN AT HER
LITTLE DEER HOOVES FEELING SHOCKED
THAT HER SPELL HAD BACKFIRED.
SHE SANG SADLY,
"ME A DEER, A FEMALE DEER?
OH DEAR, WHAT HAVE I DONE?"

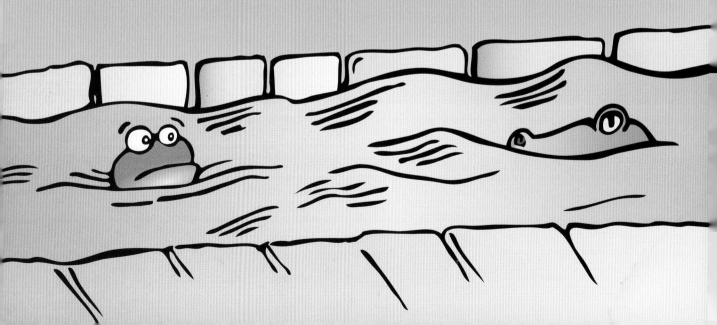

UPON HEARING HER CHANGE OF HEART
QUEEN SPELL WAS FILLED WITH GLADNESS.
KNOWING MISS SPELL HAD LEARNED
HER LESSON, SHE WAVED HER MAGIC WAND.

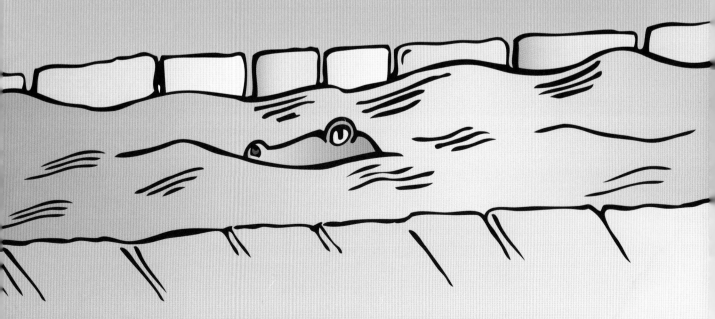

MISS SPELL POOFED BACK
INTO A LITTLE PRINCESS AGAIN
WITH A BIG JOB TO DO!

MISS SPELL PEDALED HER TRIKE DOWN THE WINDING HILL AND RODE AROUND THE VILLAGE RIGHTING HER SPELLS.

Acknowledgments

To Kate Matott, our family's
real princess! Thank you for casting
a spell of true love on Jay J!
J.M.

To all of you who have red Miss Spell,
I hope it has been an enjoyable and enlightening experience.
D.S.

This is a work of fiction, but Miss Spell is totally real!

Text copyright © 2014 by Justin Matott
Cover, Jacket and Interior illustrations Illustrations copyright © 2014 by David Schiedt
Jacket and Book Design by Amanda Lindemann, Creative Direction by David Schiedt.
Prepress, layout, and final art by Amanda Lindemann
www.busteryorkcreative.com

Permissions Department, SKOOB BOOKS,
P. O. Box 631183
Littleton, CO 80163.
Library of Congress Cataloging-in-Publication Data

MISS SPELL written by Justin Matott.
Illustrations by David Schiedt - 1st ed. p. cm. Edition
Summary: ISBN 978-1-889191-38-6 {1. picture book series. I. David Schiedt - ill. II. Title
First edition
A B C D E

To contact Justin Matott regarding his work,
please see his website at www.justinmatott.com.
For David Schiedt go to www.busteryorkcreative.com

Printed in the USA